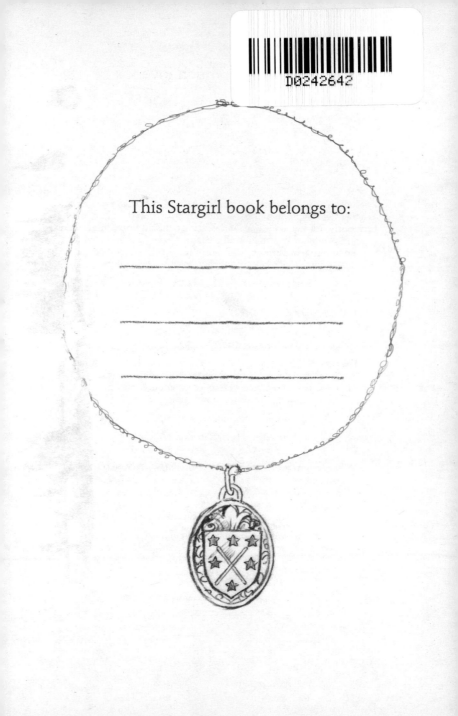

This Stargirl book belongs to:

_____

_____

_____

For Kitty, with much love x x x

First published 2013 by Walker Books Ltd
87 Vauxhall Walk, London SE11 5HJ

2 4 6 8 10 9 7 5 3 1

Text © 2013 Vivian French
Illustrations © 2013 Jo Anne Davies

The right of Vivian French and Jo Anne Davies to be identified as author and illustrator respectively of this work has been asserted by them in accordance with the Copyright, Designs and Patents Act 1988

This book has been typeset in StempelSchneidler

Printed and bound in Great Britain
by Clays Ltd, St Ives plc

British Library Cataloguing in Publication Data:
a catalogue record for this book is available from
the British Library

ISBN 978-1-4063-4938-2

www.walker.co.uk

Stargirl Academy

Melody and Jackson's Christmas Spell

VIVIAN FRENCH

WALKER
BOOKS

HEAD TEACHER
Fairy Mary McBee

DEPUTY HEAD
Miss Scritch

TEACHER
Fairy Fifibelle Lee

TEAM STARLIGHT

Lily

Madison

Sophie

Ava

Emma

Olivia

TEAM TWINSTAR

Melody

Jackson

Dear Stargirl,

Welcome to *Stargirl Academy*!

My name is Fairy Mary McBee, and I'm delighted you're here. All my Stargirls are very special, and I can tell that you are wonderful too.

We'll be learning how to use magic safely and efficiently to help anyone who is in trouble, but before we go any further I have a request. The Academy MUST be kept secret. This is VERY important...

So may I ask you to join our other Stargirls in making The Promise? Read it – say it out loud if you wish – then sign your name on the bottom line.

Thank you so much ... and well done!

Fairy Mary

The Promise

I will never speak of
Stargirl Academy to others
outside these cloudy walls,
whatever they ask and
whatever they offer.
This I solemnly promise,
for now, always
and for ever.

_____

The Book of Spells

by
Fairy Mary McBee

Head Teacher at

The Fairy Mary McBee
Academy for Stargirls

◆ ◆ ◆

A complete list of Spells can be obtained from the Academy.

Only the fully qualified need apply. Other applications

will be refused.

There are many types of spell. The six
main varieties are:

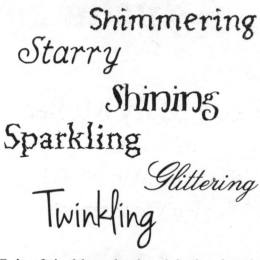

Shimmering

Starry

Shining

Sparkling

Glittering

Twinkling

It is advisable to begin with the simplest
of spells, and progress at a steady pace.
This will avoid unfortunate mistakes.
Additional spells may be added to the
programme on special occasions.

Hi! I'm Melody Ann Georgina Weston. I'm tall for my age and I'm very pretty; my best friend, Jackson, is almost as pretty as me, but not quite. I'm dark and she's fair, so we set each other off brilliantly and people stare at us when we're together, which we usually are—

Hang on a minute! What do you mean – you're prettier?

That was Jackson, and she's not supposed to interrupt. We agreed that we'd do one chapter each, and we tossed to see who'd go first and I won, so I can say what I like … but if it'll keep her quiet, I'll agree that she *is* really pretty. We've been friends for ages, and we don't take much notice of other kids, and we do what we want to do … at least, we used to. We go to Stargirl Academy now, and that makes everything different.

This is what you should know about me, Jackson and Stargirl Academy.

1. The Academy used to train Fairy Godmothers, but the head teacher, Fairy Mary McBee, decided that was old-fashioned. She thought it would be better to train girls like me and Jackson instead. The idea is that we learn how to help people, like Fairy Godmothers used to. We can't grant wishes, though. I think that's a shame.

2. We get a Tingle in our elbow when it's time to go to the Academy … and however long we're there, it doesn't matter. When we get back, it's exactly the same time as when we left.

3. We learn magic and spells. Every time we go to the Academy, they teach us a new spell, and then we try it out on a mission. We each have a magic necklace with a pendant, and on the pendant are six stars. If we do well and manage to help someone, one of the stars lights up. When we have SIX stars, we'll have finished our training, and we'll be proper Stargirls.

4. Jackson and I (we're Team Twinstar) have five stars each, but the other team – Team Starlight – has six already.

5. When Team Starlight were given their sixth star, Jackson and I felt DREADFUL. Really, REALLY dreadful.

Why?

This is where I tell you a secret about me and Jackson. It might make you not like us very much, but it's just the way we are.

Right from the very first moment we walked into the Academy, we thought we were better than the other kids... I don't suppose they're actually much younger than us, but it felt as if they were. We were totally and utterly shocked when they were given their fifth star, and we weren't. It was horrible. And then they got their final stars ... and we didn't.

Ouch.

And this is me, Jackson Williams. Best friend of Melody Ann Georgina Weston. Sometimes she says really stupid things, but she's right about the stars. It felt awful when Team Starlight started jumping about and being pleased with themselves and we were left out. I suppose it made it worse knowing that it was our fault ... we do like being different, and sometimes it gets us into trouble. The other girls are nice – don't get me wrong – but Melody and I have never quite fitted in. They're just a little bit more fluffy bunny than we are—

You mean they're nicer!

No, I don't! Well ... I suppose maybe I do. But not everyone can be sweet and kind and helpful all the time. Miss Scritch, the deputy head at Stargirl Academy, isn't. Sometimes she can be really chilly, but I have a feeling she quite likes me and Mel because we're more like her than the others are. I don't think I've ever seen any of Team Starlight slam a door or smash something because they're angry. I know I've done that, and so has Melody. And, if I'm being absolutely truthful, sometimes I find myself thinking the other Stargirls are a bunch of goody goodies. Especially when they're all together.

It's not so bad when they're on their own. Ava and Madison can be quite sparky and fun, and Lily's OK too. Emma makes me laugh because she talks so much, but

Olivia and Sophie are weird – Olivia in particular. She's scared of loads of stuff, and at first me and Melody thought she was a total wimp, but actually she thinks about other people all the time, and that freaks me out. What makes it worse is that we should be grateful, because it was Olivia who suggested that Team Starlight came back to the Academy so we could try and win our last star.

I'm sure if Fairy Mary McBee knew how we were feeling she'd chuck us out. I don't think a proper Stargirl ought to wish another Stargirl would stamp their feet and scream and shout just to show they're human—

Hadn't you better get on with the story?

Go away! I only interrupted you once, and you've done it twice now!

Sorry … You can have the first chapter.

OK. Thanks. It seemed like AGES after our last visit to the Academy before we got another Tingle. I'd almost convinced myself we were never going back, and we'd never get to be proper Stargirls. Melody thought the same, I know, although we didn't talk about it much. Mostly we pretended that we didn't care. We did, though. There's something about Stargirl Academy that gets under your skin, even if you don't want it to. And another thing – I'd discovered I was really good at magic, and I kept wondering, what if I never got to do magic again? It didn't help that it was nearly

Christmas, and everyone we met was wildly excited ... but then it finally happened.

Chapter One

My mum was working, so Melody's mum said she'd take us shopping, but she took us to the local shopping mall instead of anywhere exciting. She spent ages and AGES in every single shop making up her mind which presents to buy and we got really bored.

We moped around waiting for her to come out of the chemist, and because we had nothing else to do we watched a line of snotty-nosed kids queueing to see Father Christmas in the most unlikely grotto ever. It was a kind of cuckoo clock covered in sparkly pink fur; even Father C looked a bit embarrassed. A small scowly grown-up dressed as a silver cuckoo popped out and shouted, "Cuckoo, cuckoo! Wishes granted! Hurry up!" each time it was a kid's turn to go and collect his present; some of the tiny ones looked terrified.

"Darling, I want you to hold Baby's hand!" a mum said. I thought she was talking to me, but when I turned to glare at her – who did she think she was? – I saw she was talking to a little girl in a fussy pink velvet dress. "Hold his hand, Pipsy, and you can see Father Christmas together."

Pipsy shook her head. "But I don't want a present from here, Mumsy. I want the purple fluffy dog that runs in circles and sings – the one in the toyshop!" She grabbed at her mother's coat sleeve. "Please, Mumsy wumsy! I'll be the goodest girl in the whole wide world! I'll hold Baby's hand for ever and ever if I can have the fluffy dog! Pleeeeeease!"

 22

Mel leant over to whisper in my ear. "Mumsy wumsy? Whoever calls their mum that?"

"Whiney little girls in prissy pink dresses," I whispered back.

Pipsy was still hanging onto her mother's coat. "Please please PLEEEEASE?"

"Hush, Pipsy!" I think the mum had noticed us listening. "You can have the fluffy dog later."

"Really?" Pipsy stared at her. "The purple fluffy dog? The one that sings?"

"Of course, darling." Mumsy began hauling Baby out of his buggy. "We'll buy whatever you want. But take Baby to get his present first. He just LOVES Father Christmas, don't you, Baby? And we're going to see two Father Christmasses today, aren't we, poppet?"

"Yes," said Baby. He had a round pink face, and was already clutching an armful of toys. "Baby's going to get presents. LOTS of presents."

 24

I nudged Melody. "Spoiled brats," I said under my breath.

Melody nodded. "Look how many bags their mum's got!"

"What would you want if you could have a wish?" I asked as Mel and I moved away from Mumsy and her horrible children.

Melody shrugged. "Dunno. What about you?"

I gave her a sideways look. "I was kind of hoping I'd be a Stargirl by now..."

"Oh!" Mel took my arm. "Wouldn't it be fantastic if we won our final star in time for Christmas?"

"It'd be perfect," I said, but then we were interrupted.

A skinny woman suddenly appeared from behind the furry cuckoo clock. She barged past me and tried to pull two children away from the back of the queue, but the little girl started yelling at the top of her voice. "Nooooo! Nooooo! I want to see Santa Claus!"

Her older brother clutched at the side of the clock. "But we always come, Mum! Always!"

 26

"WAAAAAAAAHH!" screeched the girl. "WAAAAAAAH!"

The woman grabbed them, and hauled them to one side. "Joe! Jenny! I've been looking for you EVERYWHERE! I said we WEREN'T going to see Father Christmas. I TOLD you!" She was shouting so loudly I should think everyone in the mall must have heard her.

The little girl was almost purple, she was bawling so hard, but her brother was very pale.

"Why not?" he whispered, and he was obviously trying not to cry.

His mother began dragging them towards the door. "Costs too much," she snapped. She tilted her head towards a sign above the clock. It said: LET FATHER CHRISTMAS GRANT YOUR CHRISTMAS WISH! PAY THE CUCKOO AND ENTER THE MAGICAL CLOCK! ONLY £5 PER CHILD. "Waste of good money. Besides, I'm

late for work, and it's a big day at The Nag's Head. Come ON, kids..."

The boy didn't say anything else, but I saw him silently rubbing at his face with the back of his hand as he and his shrieking sister disappeared in amongst the Christmas shoppers.

"She was really mean," Melody said indignantly. "She nearly pulled their arms off! And all they wanted was one little present."

"I know," I agreed, and I thought of the parcels my mum had already started piling under our tree at home, and the way she gave me a little wink every time she saw me looking. "Do you think they'll get any presents at all?"

Melody shook her head. "Not with a mum like that. I'm sure she doesn't look after them properly. Their clothes were really tatty – and the little boy was as thin as a pin. I bet they're half-starved so their mum can have loads and

loads of wonderful clothes and chocolate and cake."

I wasn't so sure about that. The woman had been thin too, and her coat very ordinary, but when I said as much to Melody she snorted.

"Rubbish, Jackson! You heard the way she talked to them, didn't you?"

"Yes," I said.

Melody looked very serious. "If ever we get to go back to the Academy, I want to help kids like that. Poor little things! I'm sure they need help just as much as any of our friends and relations – probably a whole lot more. Have you noticed that Team Starlight always seems to choose people they know?" She sighed. "Wouldn't it be nice to be able to show them the proper way to be a Stargirl—"

And that was when the Tingle came. It was so strong it made me jump, and Melody clutched

30

her elbow at exactly the same time.

"Ouch!" she said. And then, "WOW!"

"This'll be our chance!" I knew I was right. "Our big chance!"

"Team Twinstar – the best Stargirls ever!" said Melody. And then she stopped, and we stared at each other.

We'd had the Tingle, but where did we go to find the Academy? We were right in the middle of a huge shopping mall!

"I know!" Melody slipped her arm through mine. She was grinning a wicked grin. "Come on!" And before I could say a word, she was marching me up to the pink furry cuckoo clock, pushing past the startled cuckoo, waltzing me inside ... and in through the front door of The Fairy Mary McBee Academy for Stargirls.

Chapter Two

We were still giggling at the cuckoo's expression as we walked down the hall.

"Did you hear him?" Jackson chortled. "*No no no no no* – he actually SOUNDED like a cuckoo!"

"He wasn't nice to the little kids," I said. "I saw him push a couple of them when they wouldn't go in."

Jackson shook her head. "NOT very Christmassy." And then we opened the workroom door.

I don't think Jackson told you about the Academy workroom. There's a long wooden table with twelve chairs, and that's where we sit when we're learning about magic and spells. The walls are covered in shelves and cupboards, and we've never discovered all the things that are kept there – the labels don't mean anything. There's a cupboard marked "Nine-legged spiders," and Sophie and Olivia were terrified they'd get out and crawl round the room until one day Fairy Fifibelle Lee opened it – and all that was inside was a tottering pile of old notebooks. But, on the other hand, a shelf labelled "Not Very Sharp Pencils" is weighed down with weird-looking pots and bottles with mysterious little wormy things inside. I once asked Miss Scritch what they were for, and she gave me a chilly stare and said it was highly unlikely that I'd ever need them. "Unless you intend

 34

to catch the bubonic plague, Melody?"

As well as the shelves and cupboards there are heaps of papers and ancient books, and bunches of herbs hanging from the ceiling – at least, I think they're herbs. Fairy Mary McBee has a very VERY tall sister called Fairy Prim and when she comes to visit she's always brushing her head against them, and I did notice one time that her hair was strangely green afterwards. It didn't last, though.

We were surprised to find the workroom empty ... apart from the usual clutter, of course. A small Christmas tree decorated with silver bells and twinkly lights was standing in a corner, but there wasn't a sign of any of our teachers or any of the other Stargirls.

Jackson looked around doubtfully. "We

 35

DID get a Tingle, didn't we?"

"Of course we did," I said. "And we wouldn't have got through the cuckoo clock and found ourselves here in the Academy if we hadn't been expected."

Jackson snorted. "We'd probably be sitting on Father Christmas's knee, asking for a new dolly!"

"We'll just have to wait," I said. "Maybe we're early? Or maybe Fairy Mary wants to talk to us before the others get here." I looked up at the wall where Fairy Mary McBee's special wand always hung. It was shining with a faint golden light, and I wondered what would happen when it was time for the Spin. That's when we find out who is going to lead the day's adventure, and try out the new spell that we've learnt. I crossed my fingers inside my pocket. SURELY it had

36

to be me or Jackson? After all, *we* were the
ones that needed an extra star...

Jackson saw me looking at the wand, and
went towards it. For a moment, I thought
she was going to lift it down, but she didn't.
She just touched it, very gently. "Let it be
one of us," she whispered. "PLEASE!"

"You'll have to wait and see, Jackson my pet," said a squeaky little voice. "The wand makes its own decisions!"

We stared round, but we couldn't see anyone.

Jackson nudged me. "It's coming from under the table," she said.

We bent down to peer into the shadows – and there was the tiniest fairy we'd ever seen waving up at us.

Jackson gasped as she suddenly realised who we were looking at. "It's Fairy Fifibelle Lee!" she said. "It is, isn't it?"

Fairy Fifibelle gave a peal of bell-like laughter. "Indeed it is, my darling!" She scuttled out, and stood leaning on Jackson's shoe. "Now, can you guess what spell you're going to learn today?"

My heart began to beat wildly in my chest.

"We're going to learn how to be tiny?"

Fairy Fifibelle nodded. "Shrinking and Growing, my little honey bees. Shrinking and—"

There was a shimmer of stars, a whoosh-ing noise, and Jackson gave a speedy leap backwards. Fairy Fifibelle Lee, all her gauzy scarves fluttering, was standing right in front of her.

"Wow!" We were both so amazed we couldn't think of anything else to say.

Fairy Fifibelle looked pleased. "It DID work rather well, didn't it, my sweets? It's sometimes a little tricky to grow back again. Takes more concentration, I think you'll find."

Jackson and I looked at each other. Learning how to shrink and grow sounded interesting, I thought, but Jackson said, "Just a minute. Why do we need to be tiny? We can always be invisible if we don't want people to see us," and she fingered her magic necklace. We've all got one; tap it twice and nobody can see you – except for the other Stargirls, of course, and our teachers. And even then we look sort of floaty, and almost see-through.

"Sometimes being invisible isn't enough,

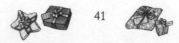

darling Jackson." Fairy Fifibelle smiled in a mysterious way. "Wait and see."

Jackson frowned. She finds Fairy Fifibelle really irritating; she says she isn't Fairy Fifibelle Lee's precious petal, or her sweetie pie, and most of the time I think the same. On the other hand, Fairy Fifibelle is surprisingly good at magic – although it does go a bit wrong sometimes. I quite like that. It makes me laugh.

"Where are the others?" I asked. "Are they coming soon?"

Fairy Fifibelle Lee put her hand to her ear. "I'd say they've just arrived," she told me, and the very next minute the door burst open and Team Starlight came tumbling into the room.

Chapter Three

I was pleased to see the rest of the Stargirls, because it meant we could get on, but they were all giggling and holding hands and my first thought was, They're so BABYISH! Then I caught myself thinking it, and I knew that wasn't the way a Stargirl ought to feel, so I did my best to smile.

"Hi, Jackson!" Emma was beaming at me. "Are you looking forward to Christmas?"

I shrugged. "Sort of."

"I can't wait," she enthused. "I absolutely love this time of year ... everyone's so happy!"

I thought of the cross man dressed up as a cuckoo, and the way he'd told the kids to hurry

43

up. And the mum who hadn't let her little girl have a present from Santa Claus. And her poor skinny brother … and the horribly spoilt Baby and Pipsy.

"Not everyone," I said. "It seems to make some people really mean."

Emma looked disappointed for a moment, but then she smiled again. "It's AGES since we were all here. I thought we were never going to get another Tingle! But we had to, didn't we, because you two need to get your last star."

"Thanks for reminding us," Melody said.

Emma blushed. "I didn't mean…" she began.

But Melody interrupted her. "It's OK. Jackson and I know why we're here. And…" She hesitated, and I could tell she was doing her best to be nice. "Thanks for coming to help us."

That nearly made me laugh, because Melody sounded as if she was making such a

mammoth effort, but Fairy Fifibelle Lee waved
her wand and sent hundreds of tiny little pink
stars twinkling round the room.

"Well said, Melody. A true Stargirl is always grateful for the help of others! And I'm sure Emma and ALL of Team Starlight will do everything they can to help you and Jackson get your final star." She stopped to wave her wand again, and the tiny pink stars went whirling round Melody's head. "Isn't that right, my honey blossoms?"

Emma beamed, but Ava gave me a tiny wink from behind Fairy Fifibelle's back, and I saw Madison roll her eyes. It's just as well they did, as I can't bear it when Fairy Fifibelle goes all hippy-dippy and gushy.

"Melody and Jackson would be fine without us," Ava said firmly. "We're only here because we love the Academy so much. And, if they're going to learn a new spell, we'd like to learn it too."

"Quite right." Our head teacher, Fairy Mary

McBee, came bustling out of the sitting-room. "I'm so sorry to keep you waiting! Are we all here?" She glanced over her shoulder. "Miss Scritch?"

Miss Scritch followed Fairy Mary into the workroom. I noticed she only gave Fairy Fifibelle a brief nod as a hello, and it made me chuckle to myself. Sometimes I think I might turn out to be like Miss Scritch when I grow up. I'll go around despising flowery people who gush, and avoiding them as much as I can.

"Good morning, Stargirls," said Miss Scritch. "I hope you're ready for a hard day's work. It may be nearly Christmas, but that's no excuse for slacking. No excuse at all!"

Fairy Fifibelle fluttered madly. "Our precious darlings have never been lazy, dear Miss Scritch. Now, shall I begin?"

If Miss Scritch's eyebrows had risen any higher

they'd have vanished. She turned to Fairy Mary McBee. "Am I to understand that Fairy Fifibelle is teaching the girls today?"

Fairy Mary was unruffled. "Fairy Fifibelle has always been wonderfully skilled at the Shrinking Spell. Perhaps you might care to take over when it comes to Growing again? That has presented problems in the past, and I'm sure Fairy Fifibelle won't mind my saying as much." She patted Fairy Fifibelle's arm, and went to fetch a pile of paper from one of the cupboards.

Fairy Fifibelle Lee clapped her hands, and beamed at Miss Scritch. "But I've just done it!" She gave me and Melody a soppy smile. "You saw my Growing Spell, didn't you, poppets?"

Melody nodded.

Fairy Fifibelle clapped her hands again, like a child who thinks it's done something terribly clever. Then she put her head on one side and

49

gazed at me. "And it worked perfectly, didn't it, my precious petal?"

There was a pause. I hate "precious petal" even more than "sweetie pie." But I was trying to be a proper Stargirl, so I said, "Yes, Fairy Fifibelle."

Chapter Four

I didn't hear what Jackson said to Fairy Fifibelle. Ava and Madison were asking me about the Shrinking Spell.

"Fairy Fifibelle was TEENY," I told them.

"Really?" Miss Scritch had heard me. "I hope you didn't raise any false expectations, Fairy Fifibelle Lee."

Fairy Fifibelle went pink. "I might have shrunk just a little bit more than I should," she confessed, and Miss Scritch gave a disapproving sniff.

"How small will we be?" Ava asked.

"About half your usual height," Fairy Mary said. "Shrinking too small can be

 51

dangerous, as I'm sure you can imagine."

Miss Scritch nodded. "Very dangerous indeed. Imagine if you were ten centimetres tall, and you met a cat!"

Olivia, looking rather pale, went to sit beside Sophie at the table, and I saw them whispering together.

Fairy Mary noticed them as well. "Don't worry, my dears," she said. "Fairy Fifibelle will show you the spell, and then we'll have a little practise to make sure you know just what to do."

Miss Scritch started to say something, but Fairy Mary McBee held up her hand. "Let it be a surprise, dear Miss Scritch," she said.

We looked at each other. A surprise? What did she mean?

Before we had time to discuss it, Fairy Fifibelle Lee moved to the head of the table.

"My darlings! I'd like you to work in pairs, if you would be so kind."

Jackson and I shuffled our chairs closer together, Madison winked at Ava, Lily grinned at Emma, and Olivia and Sophie linked arms.

"Now," Fairy Fifibelle went on, "I'd like you to make a list of the ten smallest things you can think of."

Miss Scritch coughed. "Would you like me to hand out some paper?"

"Oh yes!" Fairy Fifibelle gave a little laugh. "Silly me."

We took our piece of paper, and started our list. We began with mice, and ended with a grain of sand. Miss Scritch looked over our shoulders, and frowned. "That's much too small," she said. "If you try for that kind of

 53

size, there's a danger you'll shrink so fast you'll disappear completely."

We stared at her. "What would happen then?" I asked.

Miss Scritch sniffed. "Fairy Mary and I would have to waste a great deal of time and magic putting it right."

Sophie had overheard, and she leant towards us. "But you would be able to get us back to our normal size, wouldn't you?"

"If we could find you." Miss Scritch sniffed again. "Once a person has disappeared, it's exceedingly difficult to find them as their voices disappear with them. This is not a spell for amateurs."

Olivia gave a gasp of horror. "We'd DISAPPEAR?"

Sophie's eyes were as round as saucers. "We're not going to do that, though, are we?"

Miss Scritch cleared her throat. "Fairy

Fifibelle," she said, "I think you should get on with the Shrinking Spell. You're making Sophie and Olivia nervous."

"Oh! Oh, my poor, poor darlings!" Fairy Fifibelle rushed to hug Olivia and Sophie in a flurry of floating scarves. "You mustn't be worried!" She turned to the rest of us. "Have you all made your lists, petals?"

There was a chorus of agreement, and Fairy Fifibelle smiled. "Now, listen very carefully. Repeat after me…

> *I wish to shrink,*
> *To grow quite small.*
> *I wish to be*
> *A metre tall…*

And while you're reciting the spell, think about all the small things on your list."

 56

We nodded, and when Fairy Fifibelle said the spell again, we repeated it word for word. We did it three times ... but nothing happened. None of us shrank. Not even an inch.

"Has something gone wrong, Fairy Fifibelle?" Ava asked.

Fairy Fifibelle was looking puzzled. "It's very strange," she said. "I've never known it take so long."

Miss Scritch gave a meaningful cough. She didn't suggest anything, though, until Fairy Fifibelle dropped her wand with a clatter and said, "What could have gone wrong? You've all recited the spell perfectly." She sighed loudly.

"It's quite simple," Miss Scritch said smugly. "The girls need to have made a second list. No Shrinking magic will work unless careful preparations have been made

 57

for reversing the spell afterwards."

Fairy Fifibelle Lee blushed. "Oh, silly SILLY me!"

Before Miss Scritch could agree – and I could see that she was bursting to – Fairy Mary said quietly, "Don't worry, Fairy Fifibelle. We all make mistakes. It's an important part of every Stargirl's education to learn that making mistakes can teach her far more than getting everything right all the time. Isn't that so, Jackson?"

Chapter Five

Fairy Mary looked straight at me as she spoke, and it made me jump.

"Erm ... yes," I said, and I had an uneasy feeling that she meant something in particular.

"Nobody ever learnt anything of value without overcoming a problem or two first." Fairy Mary went on, and now she was talking to all of us. "It's something we must all remember. Fairy Fifibelle, do go on with your lesson."

Fairy Fifibelle had recovered, and she handed us each another sheet of paper with her usual smile. "Darlings – another list. This time, the ten biggest things you can think of. Mountains, castles ... whatever you like."

 59

This one was simple. Melody began with an elephant, and I finished up with Cloudy Towers – that's the old name for the Academy, because it's built on a cloud, and has so many towers you can't count them all. Once we'd finished, Fairy Fifibelle asked us to put our pieces of paper on the floor.

"Why the floor?" Emma asked.

"You'll soon see, dearest Emma." Fairy Fifibelle gave her a meaningful smile. "Now, my sweets, please try the spell again. Forget the list you've just made, and think about the small things."

"May I make a suggestion?" Miss Scritch leant forward. "Girls! Leave your chairs, and close your eyes before trying the spell."

Fairy Fifibelle frowned. "Thank you, Miss Scritch. I was just about to tell the girls to do exactly that."

"Excellent." Miss Scritch sat back, and

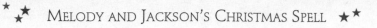

watched as we went to stand in a row by the wall, closed our eyes, and began to chant the spell.

> "I wish to shrink,
> To grow quite small.
> I wish to be
> A metre tall…"

It was the weirdest feeling I've ever had in my entire life. I could actually feel myself shrinking … and it wasn't very nice. My legs and arms felt prickly all over, and for a moment or two my tongue felt too big for my mouth … but then it seemed to settle. I could hear Melody gasp, so I opened my eyes – and I gasped too. We'd shrunk! Really and truly! Our noses were level with the table, and Fairy Fifibelle Lee and Miss Scritch and Fairy Mary looked ENORMOUS!

There were twinkly stars floating in the air above our heads, but as I looked up at them they faded away.

"Jeepers creepers!" Lily was staring down at her skirt. "EVERYTHING'S shrunk! Even our clothes!"

Fairy Mary chuckled. "Just as well, dear. Think what would happen if they stayed the same size!"

That made Sophie, Emma, Madison and Ava hoot with laughter. Olivia didn't even smile; she was rubbing her arms in an anxious kind of way. "I do feel peculiar," she said.

"That's because you are," I told her. I thought she'd laugh, but she didn't. She gave me one of her wide-eyed looks.

"I know," she said.

I sighed. "I was joking. You know? Funny ha ha?"

"That's enough, Jackson!" Miss Scritch

snapped. "And I'm sorry, Olivia. Fairy Fifibelle Lee should have warned you that sensitive people often feel uncomfortable. If you wish to be excused from trying again, I will understand. Now, I think we'll try the Growing Spell. Can you all read your lists? The ones on the floor?"

Emma was positively wriggling with excitement. "Oh! NOW I understand! If we shrank even a little bit more, we wouldn't have been able to see them on the table!"

"This is where you have to concentrate." Miss Scritch folded her arms. "Think of ALL the things on your list – the mountains and the elephants – and repeat after me...

> I wish to grow,
> To make things right.
> I wish to be
> My normal height!"

"Do we shut our eyes again?" Ava asked.

"Of course." Miss Scritch tapped her fingers on the table. "Everybody ready? Right! Repeat the spell after me!"

We did as we were told, and I'd hardly said the last word before I could feel a weird sensaton, as if my legs were stretching … and my arms as well. My head buzzed, and my ears popped – and I heard Miss Scritch say, "Goodness! That is quite remarkable! QUITE remarkable!"

I opened my eyes, and found I was my usual height … but I was the only one. The other Starguls still had their eyes screwed up, and were muttering the spell over and over.

Fairy Mary gave me a congratulatory smile. "Well done, Jackson. You have a real gift for magic." She hesitated, and then went on, "Please remember that it IS a gift, and use it well."

"Yes, Fairy Mary," I said.

Fairy Fifibelle was gazing at me. "Jackson darling! What a wonderful WONDERFUL thing!"

I thought she was going to float across and hug me, so I hastily pointed at Emma. "Is Emma OK? It looks as if she's getting smaller, not taller."

Fairy Fifibelle was immediately distracted, and she rushed to Emma's side. "Think LARGE, Emma dear! Think MOUNTAINS, poppet!"

Miss Scritch frowned. "She can manage perfectly well on her own," she said.

But Fairy Fifibelle must have had some effect because Emma gave a little squeak, and shot up right in front of us. It was the most extra-ordinary thing to watch. One minute she was the height of the table, and the next she was – I can't think of the right word. Lengthening,

 66

perhaps – and then there she was, looking as if she'd never changed at all.

"Wow," Emma said, and grabbed the back of a chair to steady herself. "That was like whizzing up in the fastest lift ever!"

"Do you feel all right, dear?" Fairy Mary asked.

Emma nodded. "I feel fine. Just a bit dizzy. But I did it, didn't I?"

She sounded SO pleased with herself. I started to point out that she hadn't exactly done it on her own, but I caught Fairy Mary's eye. She made me feel a little bit uncomfortable, so I shrugged, and let Emma go on thinking she was a total star.

Chapter Six

Jackson's always been better at magic than the rest of us. It took me several goes to grow back to my normal height, but I still beat Team Starlight, except for Emma, and she had help from Fairy Fifibelle. Miss Scritch had to help Olivia, and she moaned all the time she was growing. "Fusspot," I thought, but I didn't say anything.

Once we were all sitting around the table again, Fairy Mary leant forward. "Dear Stargirls," she said, "that was a difficult spell. You are to be congratulated. Now, I think we should have a little break." She turned to Miss Scritch. "I'd say it was

time for our surprise, wouldn't you, Miss
Scritch?"

Miss Scritch pulled her wand out of
her pocket. "As you wish, Fairy Mary."
She waved the wand in the air … and we
jumped. Shining stars whizzed round and
round the ceiling, and a bright red cloth
patterned with snowflakes floated down
onto the table.

"A Christmas feast! DO let me help!"
Fairy Fifibelle stretched out her arms, and
hundreds of toy-sized knives and forks
clattered out of a cupboard and flew through
the air before landing in front of Miss Scritch
in a tangled heap. Seconds later, a pile of at
least fifty tiny tea plates wobbled down
from the ceiling and landed with a crash,
smashing into smithereens.

Fairy Fifibelle looked most surprised.

70

"That's very strange," she said. "I've never known that happen before." She waved her arms again, and a cascade of teeny weeny hot sausage rolls poured down from nowhere.

Just before they swamped the table, Miss Scritch gave a sharp "Tut!" and snapped her fingers. At once, the scattered bits of china and the sausage rolls vanished. I was sorry to see the sausage rolls go; Jackson and I hadn't had any lunch, and I was hungry.

Fairy Fifibelle frowned, but Fairy Mary put a gentle hand on her shoulder. "Thank you, Fairy Fifibelle," she said. "I think the magic from your Shrinking Spell is still lingering around you. Why don't you let Miss Scritch arrange things, just for now."

Miss Scritch gave a barely disguised snort, and twitched her wand. This time a pile of

normal-sized plates landed neatly on the table, together with a tray of mince pies sprinkled with sugar frosting, and a huge jug of cream. Then came an enormous Christmas cake decorated with snowmen and robins, and that was followed by a large bowl of hot sausage rolls.

"Sausage rolls?" Miss Scritch raised her eyebrows. "I don't remember ordering those!"

"It was me," Fairy Mary told her. "Melody looked so disappointed when the other ones vanished. I don't think an extra treat will do any harm."

Judging by the speed with which the sausage rolls vanished for a second time (and NO magic involved) I wasn't the only Stargirl who was hungry. The mince pies were popular too, and once we'd tasted the rich fruity Christmas cake, none of us could resist a second slice. Mugs of frothy hot chocolate flavoured with cinnamon and heaped with whipped cream and marshmallows appeared just when we thought we couldn't manage another mouthful ... and suddenly it seemed that we could, after all.

"Jeepers creepers." Lily sighed with pleasure as she put down her empty

mug. "I'm so full it hurts. That cake was absolutely SCRUMPTIOUS!"

Miss Scritch almost smiled. "I'm glad you enjoyed it, Lily."

"Oh, I did!" Lily leant back in her seat. "I don't think I'll ever be able to move again."

"I do hope that's not true, dear," Fairy Mary said. "We're about to have the Spin, and after that you'll be going to see who you can help." She gave a tiny sigh. "It won't be difficult. You'll find a great many people need extra help at Christmas."

I thought of the two children waiting in the queue at Santa's grotto, and how their mother had hauled them away without a present. I imagined them crouched in front of an empty fireplace with no Christmas dinner, while their horrible mother shouted

 74

at them, and I decided that if the Golden Wand pointed at me I'd do my very best to help them. Team Starlight always helped people they knew, but that was too easy. I was certain it would be MUCH better to help strangers. Wasn't that what Fairy Godmothers did in the olden days? And weren't we meant to be modern-day Fairy Godmothers?

I was about to ask Jackson if she'd do the same if the wand pointed at her, but I didn't get the chance. Fairy Mary had already put the wand on the table, and everyone was silent.

It's strange how that happens when it's time for the Spin. It's not the silence you get when nobody speaks, but a kind of expectant hush, as if even the walls of the room are waiting for something. The light

dims as well, and only the wand glows as Fairy Mary sets it spinning.

Fairy Mary looked round at us. "Dear Stargirls … as you well know, whoever the wand chooses will decide what will happen next, and who they'd like to help. Now, let us begin."

She leant forward, and blew very gently … and at once the wand began to twirl round and round making a soft humming sound. Twinkling stars floated up and hovered over our head teacher's head as she murmured, "Spin, spin, spin. Who will choose? Who will it be? Whose destiny will change to-day? Spin, wand, spin."

The wand spun, and the room filled with a golden light. Everyone was gazing at the wand as it spun faster and faster and faster, and the humming grew louder and louder.

None of us moved; it was as if we were kept completely motionless by the wand's magic … and then it stopped. It didn't slow down. It stopped dead – and it was pointing exactly halfway between me and Jackson.

"Melody and Jackson," Fairy Mary said, "there's no doubt about it. The wand has chosen you both."

Chapter Seven

I think I was holding my breath all the time the wand was spinning. I was trying so hard to make it point at me or Melody my head was hurting. I kept thinking, "Please let it be one of us! We SO need to show that we can be the best! Please please please!" And when it did stop I was so relieved I let out a cheer, and everyone looked at me in astonishment because that is NOT the sort of thing I usually do. I pretended I had something wrong with my shoe and bent down so nobody could see my face until I stopped blushing.

"Well done, Melody," Madison said. "Well done, Jackson. Do you know who you're

going to help? Are we going out in the Travelling Tower?"

"Maybe," Melody said. "We did have an idea, as it happens." I knew she was just as excited as I was, but she wasn't going to show it. She turned to Fairy Mary. "Can we find someone if we don't know where they live? Jackson and I saw two children with their mum in our local shopping centre today, and they looked SO miserable. The mum wouldn't even let them get a present from Santa Claus, and I think that's terrible."

Fairy Mary looked thoughtful. "You've only seen them once. Are you sure they need your help?"

I nodded. "Their mum was shouting at them and dragging them away – she was horrible!"

"Perhaps she was worried," Miss Scritch suggested.

"No," Melody said firmly. "My mum would never behave like that, however worried she was."

I wasn't quite so certain. I once ran across a road in front of a car, and my mum yelled at me until she just about lost her voice ... but then again, she'd never drag me around in front of other people.

Fairy Fifibelle waved her arms. "Surely we should trust our precious petals?"

"You're right, Fairy Fifibelle," Fairy Mary said. "Melody, Jackson – tell us what you know about these children and their mother."

"The mum was on her way to work," Melody told her. "She was worried about being late."

I remembered something. "Yes. She said... What was it? Oh! That it was a big day at The Nag's Head. That must be where she works."

Fairy Fifibelle Lee came swooping round the table. "Darling girl! SUCH a memory!

There's the answer, my sweets – we'll take the Travelling Tower, and we'll find The Nag's Head in no time."

"What's The Nag's Head?" Ava wanted to know.

Miss Scritch looked disapproving. "I imagine it's a public house. Fairy Mary, ought we to allow the girls to go to such an establishment? It might not be at all suitable!"

"I shall take the greatest care of them," Fairy Fifibelle declared, and my heart sank. That meant she was coming with us, and I'd been hoping she wouldn't. I wanted me and Melody to be hugely successful, and when Fairy Fifibelle's around she makes such a fuss that I can't think straight. Melody and I had got things wrong once before, and a nasty secret little voice deep inside me was whispering that it could happen again...

81

"I think," Fairy Mary said slowly, "I shall go myself. Perhaps you and Miss Scritch would like to prepare the certificates ready for our return?"

That REALLY made butterflies flutter in my stomach. Supposing Melody and I didn't win our final stars after all? If we didn't, we wouldn't be fully qualified Stargirls ... and it would be very unlikely that we'd be given another chance. And, as if she'd read my thoughts, Miss Scritch asked, "Are we to prepare six certificates, Fairy Mary, or eight?"

Fairy Mary smiled one of her sunniest smiles. "Oh, I think eight. I'm sure that Melody and Jackson will win their stars this time. Isn't that right, girls?" And she looked at us as if she was absolutely certain that we would. It made me feel a whole lot better – but then Fairy Fifibelle went and ruined it. She made a cooing noise, and flung her arms around me.

"My darling honey pies always do their best," she twittered. *"But sometimes they get just a teeny bit carried away, don't you, my poppets?"*

"No," I said. *I knew it sounded rude, but I couldn't help it. What I really wanted to do was tell her,* DON'T HUG ME! *Just leave me alone! I've got something really difficult to do, and I want to get on with it! If it all goes hideously wrong I'll crawl away home, and hug my mum.*

Fairy Fifibelle Lee kept treating me and Melody as if we were babies – and I'd suddenly had enough.

I took a deep breath, but Miss Scritch interrupted before I'd even opened my mouth.

"Come along, Fairy Fifibelle," she said briskly. *"We can work next door. The sooner we begin, the sooner we'll be finished."* She took

Fairy Fifibelle's arm, and marched her towards the sitting room.

"Hm." Fairy Mary's eyes were very bright. "Jackson dear, I think Miss Scritch has just saved you from saying something you would have regretted. At least, I HOPE you would have regretted it."

I didn't know how to answer her. If Miss Scritch hadn't stopped me telling Fairy Fifibelle what I thought of her, would I really have been sorry later? I pushed my hair behind my ears while I tried to work it out. Something in Fairy Mary's blue-eyed gaze made me want to be completely truthful. "I hope so too," I said at last. "But I'm not absolutely sure I would."

I heard Olivia give a little gasp, and I waited for Fairy Mary to give me a row for being so nasty – but she didn't. Instead, she chuckled.

"Jackson Williams, sometimes you are

surprisingly honest. That is a good thing. But you do, however, need to be far more forgiving of other people, however irritating they might be." And she actually winked!

"Yes, Fairy Mary," I said. "I'll try." And I meant it. When someone's as nice as Fairy Mary, it makes you really want to do your best – and not just because you want to win a star. You don't want to let them down. And I didn't want to let myself down, either. Or Melody.

"Good. That's settled." Fairy Mary gave a little nod as if she'd sorted something, and was pleased about it. "Now, shall we see if we can find The Nag's Head, and those two children?"

Chapter Eight

We have to go through the sitting-room to get to the Travelling Tower. It's a lovely room; there's always a cosy fire burning, and the sofas and chairs are squashy and comfortable. Fairy Fifibelle Lee and Miss Scritch were settled in a corner with pens and ink and a pile of paper.

"Look!" Sophie whispered. "They're writing out our certificates! Our Stargirl certificates!"

"SO exciting," Madison agreed, "but I've just thought of something scary. What if we get things wrong today? Could we have a star taken away from us?"

"Jeepers creepers!" Lily stopped so suddenly that Sophie and Ava and Olivia very nearly crashed into her. "Do you think that could happen?"

Miss Scritch looked up from her corner. "Indeed it could."

"Oh!" Lily looked so shocked that I nearly laughed.

But Fairy Mary had overheard and she was smiling. "You'd have to do something very dreadful, dear. I don't think you should worry about it. Now, hurry along."

We set off again, but I could see that Team Starlight was thinking about what Miss Scritch had said. They weren't as pleased with themselves as they had been.

Good, I thought. Now they knew how Jackson and I felt. And quite soon they were going to find out that WE could help people

we didn't even know … and we found them by being observant, and on the lookout.

Emma came to walk beside me as we turned into the long corridor that leads to the Travelling Tower. "What were the children doing when you saw them? Were they very unhappy? How are we going to help them?"

"You'll see," I said. I took Jackson's arm and pulled her ahead of the others. "Listen, Jackson. What do you think of trying to do this on our own? We could tell the others to wait in the TT until we need them, then leave them there until we've sorted everything, and it's time to go home again."

I thought Jackson would agree with me, but she hesitated. "I don't think Fairy Mary would like that much," she said slowly. "She likes us to work together…"

I didn't have time to argue because we'd arrived at the Travelling Tower, and I could see the sunshine beaming in. You think you're just going into another tower when you walk through the door, but the walls are made of glass, and it's really special. The Academy itself sits on a cloud and the cloud can float us where we need to go, but the Travelling Tower zooms up and down like a lift, taking us to ground level and back again. And sometimes it goes sideways as well … and once it even went back into the past. The first time we went travelling I was scared, although I never let anyone know. Not even Jackson.

I led the way in; Fairy Mary closed the door behind us, and I saw she was carrying the Golden Wand. The others had noticed too, and Emma asked her why she'd brought it. "Isn't it terribly precious?"

"It is," Fairy Mary said, "but it's also extremely useful. Much too useful to leave hanging on a wall. Where were you when you first saw the children, Melody?"

"At the Washington Shopping Mall," I told her. "And then they were going to The Nag's Head."

Fairy Mary balanced the wand on the palm of one hand, and waved the other over it. The wand quivered, and pointed to the left.

"Excellent." Fairy Mary smiled at us. "As I said, extremely useful. Now we know which way to go."

At once the TT gave a lurch, and Olivia squealed. She nearly always makes a fuss when the Travelling Tower takes off, even though you'd think she'd be used to it by now. We sailed out into the sunshine,

92

and Jackson and I stood close to the glass looking down ... and we'd only been travelling for about ten minutes when we saw it. The Nag's Head. And I was amazed!

It wasn't in a part of town where Jackson

and I ever go. It's much too posh and boring, with wide streets and no shops for miles – but there was a pub tucked in between two of the largest houses. It was a very old building; it had those black crisscrossed beams that you see in pictures of Elizabethan times, and the chimneys were twisted and crooked. Behind it was a garden where old-fashioned wooden tables and chairs were arranged on the grass ... and as we hovered above the chimneys, we saw two children run out of the back door.

"It's them!" I said. "Look, Jackson! There they are! It's the children we saw in the shopping mall!"

Jackson nodded, and opened one of the TT's windows so we could hear what they were saying.

The children were playing tag, and the

 94

boy was laughing as he ran away from his little sister. "Can't catch me!" he called. "Can't catch me!"

"They don't exactly look unhappy," Ava said as we stared down. "Are you sure those are the right children?"

I didn't answer. I was watching as the boy dodged in and out of the tables, and his sister chased after him. "Come on, Jenny!" he shouted. "Run faster!"

And then their mother came out of the back door carrying some empty cardboard boxes. "Here we go," I thought, and I waited for her to screech at them for being so noisy. But she didn't. She put the boxes down by the bins, and I saw she was actually smiling.

"Go on, Jenny!" she said. "Catch our Joe and give him a nice big hug!"

"Can't," Jenny said. "Joe-joe's too quick. You catch him!"

The mother ran across the grass and swept the boy up into her arms. "Gotcha!" she said and she kissed the tip of his nose. "And I'm ever so sorry I was mean to you earlier. I oughtn't to have shouted like that. I was worried 'cos I didn't know where you'd gone – I never thought you'd go and

see that Santa when I'd told you not to."

Joe gave his mum a huge smile. "'S all right, Mum. I know the real Santa'll come on Christmas Eve..." For a moment he looked doubtful. "He will, won't he?"

His mum kissed him again. "Of course he will. You don't think he'd miss the two best kiddies in the whole wide world, do you?"

Joe wriggled out of his mum's arms, but

he was still smiling. "I'll tell Jenny. She really wanted to see the Santa in the mall ... she remembered you taking us last year."

"I might have guessed." Joe's mum shook her head, and sighed. "She's still too small to know how much things cost. They're ever such rubbish, those five-quid parcels. Don't you remember the lorry you got last year? It fell to pieces before you'd even got it home."

Joe nodded, and then looked around. "Where's Auntie Anna? Isn't she collecting us?"

His mum laughed. "Guess what! You know I said that I had a really busy day today? Well, the boss says you and Jenny can stay and join in!"

Joe didn't look very thrilled. "Is it old people playing bingo?"

 98

"No, it's a surprise." His mum ruffled his hair. "You'll like it, I promise! But you'll have to keep an eye on Jenny. I'll be much too busy. Now, come inside and I'll show you where you'll be sitting…"

Chapter Nine

I couldn't think of anything to say as I watched the children scampering after their mother. There was a chilly feeling in the pit of my stomach. Melody and I had been totally wrong about them. It was obvious that their mum loved them just as much as my mum loved me. Maybe it wasn't so easy helping people when you knew nothing about them?

And then I thought of something else. We'd failed before we'd even started. We hadn't found someone to help. We wouldn't get our final star, and we wouldn't ever be qualified Stargirls...

The chilly feeling in my stomach changed into a horrible leaden weight, and for a moment

I thought I was going to cry. We'd meant to be a brilliant success and prove we could be different from the others. If I'm really, truly honest, we'd wanted to show them that we were the best. MUCH the best. And Fairy Mary had said she believed in us ... but it had all gone wrong. We'd made a terrible mistake.

But then, exactly as if a light had switched on in my brain, I remembered Fairy Mary telling us we could learn more by making mistakes than if we always got everything right.

Could that be true, I wondered? If it was, then maybe, just maybe, if we stopped worrying about being the best and worked together with Team Starlight, it would be OK in the end... But how?

I turned away from Melody and the others, looked in the opposite direction – and my eyes opened wide.

 101

Walking down the road was Pipsy, and behind her was her mum pushing Baby in his buggy. Behind them was another family, and on the other side of the road were more parents and children – and they were all heading for The Nag's Head. And then I noticed the sign outside on the pavement: Children's Christmas Party! TODAY!

A tiny little hope crept into my mind, and I nudged Melody. "Look!" I whispered.

Melody swung round. She was blinking away tears, and I knew she'd been thinking the same as me – that we were failures.

"What? What is it?" She glanced down at the sign, but it didn't mean anything to her. "Jackson! What are we going to do?" she whispered, and her voice was shaky ... but my head was suddenly buzzing. I'd had another of those light-bulb moments. A really

REALLY brilliant one! We could still be the best!
ABSOLUTELY the best. We could be the best at
making a mistake and getting over it and show-
ing that we'd learnt from what had happened.
And I knew how to do it!

"It's OK," I whispered back. "I've had an
idea … but you'll have to trust me."

 103

"Melody? Jackson?" Emma was puzzled. "Are we meant to be helping those kids in the garden?"

"No," Melody said. I gave her the smallest nod, and she went on, "but Jackson knows what we're going to do. She'll tell you. Won't you, Jackson?"

"Yes." I stood up straight. "But first I want to say that I'm sorry, really sorry. Mel and I got it wrong about Jenny and Joe." I saw Madison and Ava exchange glances, and I guessed they'd worked that out for themselves. I didn't care, though. Fairy Mary was giving me the biggest, beamingest smile ever.

"So what are we going to do instead?" Sophie asked.

"I'm asking you to help us," I said. "I'm asking if you'll help us to find somebody who needs us—"

104

And then I had to stop, because there was a sudden explosion of the twinkliest little stars. The Travelling Tower was so full of them I couldn't see a thing. Something brushed against me and, just for a second, I thought I heard a voice breathing, "SUCH a clever petal." But it was so faint that I decided I must have imagined it. I was even more certain I'd imagined a "Tsk! Tsk!"

I blinked and rubbed my eyes – and the stars were gone. And there was nobody in the TT except for Fairy Mary and us Stargirls, so I knew I couldn't possibly have heard Fairy Fifibelle and Miss Scritch.

"Jeepers creepers!" Lily said. "What happened there?"

Fairy Mary shook her head. "Who knows, my dear. Jackson, I'm so sorry you were interrupted."

"It's OK," I said. "So, is that agreed? You don't mind helping us?"

Olivia stepped forward. "Of course not," she said. "We're really pleased to be asked." She looked at Sophie. "Aren't we?"

"Yes," Sophie said, and so did Ava, Lily and Emma.

"It'll be our pleasure." Madison took off her glasses, wiped them clean, put them back on

and grinned at me. "Especially as I don't think you've ever asked us for help before. Have you got any ideas about where we can begin?"

"We are all," I announced, "going to go to The Nag's Head Children's Christmas Party. Fairy Mary told us that lots of people need help at this time of year, and it's just the kind of place to find someone." I pointed out of the window. "I thought we could take the TT down into the garden, tap our pendants so we're invisible, and creep inside. Then we can shrink ourselves so we can listen and watch without bumping into anyone and scaring them—" I saw Olivia's expression, and went on, "But it would be sensible if one or two of us waited in the Travelling Tower in case of emergencies."

Olivia gave a sigh of relief.

"The rest of us can have a look round for ten minutes," I went on, "then report back on

 107

what we've seen and heard … and decide what to do."

Madison grinned. "Sounds good to me."

"Me too," said Ava. Emma and Lily nodded.

"And me," Sophie said.

Olivia gave me a grateful smile.

Chapter Ten

Sometimes I get fed up with Jackson being bossy, but sometimes she gets it really right. I'd been so certain we were going to fail that my mind had turned into mush, and I couldn't think of anything useful ... but her idea of going to the Children's Christmas Party was brilliant.

As the Travelling Tower floated down to the garden below I felt loads better, and when we landed with a gentle thud I was just as excited as Emma and Ava and Madison and Lily. Sophie and Olivia said they'd stay in the TT; Olivia didn't want to risk having to try the Shrinking Spell, and

 109

Sophie was happy to keep Olivia company.

The doors of the TT opened, and we waited for Fairy Mary to lead the way out, but she didn't. "I'm going to stay here," she said, "so there's no need for you to stay unless you wish to, Sophie dear. It's important that you Stargirls make your own decisions, and find your own way through any problems."

"I'll wait by the back door, then," Sophie said. "I might be useful as a messenger, and I'll still be near Olivia."

Olivia put her hand on Sophie's arm. "It's OK. I've decided I'm coming too. Is that all right, Fairy Mary?"

"Of course, Olivia," Fairy Mary said, "but what about the Shrinking Spell?"

"It's true. I didn't like shrinking," Olivia admitted, "but I'm a Stargirl now.

 110

And I think Stargirls should do things even if they don't like them much."

There was a curious swirling in the air as if someone or something was waving wildly. I looked at Fairy Mary, but she didn't seem to have noticed anything. She was smiling at Olivia as if she'd done something quite incredible.

The rest of us are going to shrink, but we're not making a fuss about it, I thought. But all I said was, "The more the merrier."

Jackson gave Olivia and Sophie a thumbs up. "Let's go!"

We tapped our pendants to make ourselves invisible, and tiptoed out into the garden of The Nag's Head. The grass was very wet and soggy, and when we reached the concrete path I noticed we were leaving a trail of footprints behind us.

"We'd better wipe our feet," I whispered as we stopped outside the back door.

Lily giggled. "Imagine people's faces if they saw footprints suddenly appearing out of nowhere!"

"I expect there's a mat inside," Emma said, and before any of us could stop her she put

out her hand and opened the door wide –
and we saw a group of children staring at
us. Well, not exactly *at* us, because we were
invisible, but at the door.

Jenny's mum appeared. "Who opened the door, kids?" she asked. "You're letting the cold air in!"

"It opened on its own!" said a tall boy. "I saw the handle turn, but there was nobody on the other side! Nobody! I was standing right next to it. It must have been a ghost, Mrs Gibbs!"

A couple of little girls let out a screech and rushed away, but Mrs Gibbs shook her head. "I expect it was the wind, love," she said. "It's a funny old building, but it doesn't have any ghosts. Not that I know of, anyway, and I've worked here for years." She pulled the door closed with a bang. "There! That'll keep it shut. Now, let's see what's going on, shall we? It's very nearly time for tea."

She shooed the children down the

 114

passageway, and a moment later we were on our own.

"Phew!" Jackson let out a sigh of relief. "That was tricky."

"Tricky?" I said. "It was STUPID!"

I was about to say a whole lot more, but Jackson stuck her elbow into my side. "DON'T!" she hissed.

There was a muffled sob. I swung round and there was Emma, hunched up on the cold stone floor with her face in her hands.

"I'm so sorry!" she wailed. "I didn't think what I was doing! Melody's right! I'm stupid!"

"It's OK. Don't worry about it. Nobody guessed we were here."

I could hardly believe my ears. It was Jackson who had spoken and, even more surprisingly, she went over to Emma and

put an arm round her without saying a word about how silly she'd been. "Come on," she said. "Let's go and join the party!"

Chapter Eleven

We tiptoed down the passage. As we got nearer to the open door at the far end we could hear chattering and laughing. It sounded as if the party was going really well.

Lily put her hands over her ears. "Jeepers creepers! It sounds like a MILLION children!"

"Are we going to shrink before we go in?" Sophie asked.

"Do we need to?" Emma sounded doubtful. "Couldn't we just walk round to begin with?"

"I'll go and have a look." Ava slid through the door, then shot back out again. "It's STUFFED with kids," she reported. "There's hardly room to move. There are LOADS of tables and

benches and chairs, all squeezed together."

Madison chuckled. "I used to go to parties like that when I was little. They always ended with the boys throwing buns around."

Sophie sighed. "Just like my little brother."

"If it's terribly crowded, it'll be easier if we're smaller," I said. "We'll creep under the tables."

"It's the only way we'll get to the other end of the room," Ava agreed. "Someone will notice if we try to squeeze past them."

Melody had been to have a look as well. "Unless you want to crawl across the ceiling," she said, "we'll have to shrink."

Everyone nodded, and we shut our eyes and began the spell.

"I wish to shrink,
To grow quite small.
I wish to be
A metre tall..."

And this time it was SO much easier! Even Olivia didn't have any trouble ... and it didn't feel nearly as weird as it did the first time. What WAS weird was suddenly seeing the door handle at the height of my nose, and the ceiling looking as if it was miles away.

"Right!" I said. "Let's go. We'll meet back here in ten minutes' time."

We gave each other a thumbs up, and I led the way out of the corridor.

I'd been wondering if horrible Pipsy had been making a nuisance of herself. When we got to the doorway she was the first child I saw, and I stayed where I was to see what she was up to. She was sitting at the end of one of the tables;

Joe and Jenny were at the other end, smiling and laughing. Every table had ten or eleven children sitting squashed along benches, and there was SO much food! I could see loads of different kinds of sandwiches and rolls, and there were sausages and bowls of crisps, and Mrs Gibbs and several other helpers were squeezing their way in between the tables with massive trays of pizza slices.

Baby was sitting next to Pipsy. Now I was closer I could see that he wasn't really a baby. He must have been at least three, and as Jenny's mum came nearer he started shouting, "Peeta! Peeta!"

Pipsy glared at him. "Say PLEASE, Baby!"

"Humph," I thought. "I bet SHE never says please!"

Baby took no notice of his sister. "Peeta!" he yelled. "Want PEETA!"

The children's mother came squeezing in between the tables. The mums and dads and other grown-ups were sitting in comfy armchairs at the back of the room, and she had a lot of trouble making her way through.

"Pipsy!" she said. "You're not looking after Baby!" She gave the little boy a hug. "Don't you worry, precious. Baby will have his pizza very soon." She gave Pipsy a frosty stare, and began

edging her way back to her seat.

Baby banged on the table with his spoon. "BAD Pipsy," he crowed. "Pipsy's a naughty girl! Naughty, naughty, Pipsy wipsy!"

Sophie hadn't gone with the others either. She was watching Baby, and I could tell she was shocked. "He's a horror, isn't he?" she whispered, although there was so much noise I don't think anyone would have noticed even if she'd shouted. "His poor sister! Their mum didn't even smile at her! She just told her off! Pipsy's not much older than he is, either."

"She's a spoilt little brat," I said. "She wanted a purple fluffy dog – I think it was a dog – and she nagged and nagged until her mum said she'd get it for her."

Sophie put her head on one side. "But did her mum actually buy it?" she asked.

"What?" I looked at Sophie in surprise. "I don't know... She said she was going to."

"My gran's like that." Sophie sighed. "If I ask for anything she always says, 'Yes, Sophie, dear,' just to keep me quiet, and then does

 124

nothing about it. But she absolutely adores my little brother Pete, and she gets him LOADS of stuff." She shrugged. "I don't mind now. I know it's because she's old, but when I was younger I used to get furious. She's coming to stay this Christmas, and mum and I just KNOW Pete'll be given masses of presents, and he'll get all whiney and stroppy and keep asking her for more and more and more things. And he's not really like that."

"Oh." I had another look at Pipsy. Jenny's mum had just come up to the table, and Pipsy was asking quite politely if she and her little brother could have a slice of pizza each, and Mrs Gibbs was smiling at her and saying that yes, of course she could. But when Pipsy put the pizza on her little brother's plate, he crammed it all into his mouth at once, and then grabbed her piece.

"Oi!" I said, and I took a couple of steps forward.

"Jackson!" Sophie grabbed my arm. "What are you going to do?"

I'd been about to tell Baby that he was a little pig, and I think I MIGHT have been about to snatch his plate away as well, but Sophie stopped me.

"Don't! He can't see you and you'll scare him!" she warned. "Anyway, we ought to get back to the others."

Something jabbed me in the ribs, and I realised Melody was standing beside me. "Come on," she hissed. "Everyone's waiting for you!"

Chapter Twelve

I'd been all the way round the room, and so had Ava and Emma. Lily had been really clever; she and Olivia had found some stairs leading up to a little balcony overlooking the party, and they'd been watching from up there. They said they'd had to be careful as there was a huge net full of balloons hidden from the children and there wasn't much room, but it had been a brilliant viewpoint. Madison had crept under the tables all the way to where the grown-ups were sitting.

"So," I said, as we reached the corridor, "who should we be helping?"

Madison tapped her pendant to make herself visible, and we all did the same. "It's easier if you can see who you're talking to," she said.

Ava sighed. "All the kids we saw were having a great time."

Emma was rubbing her elbows. "I could do with being even smaller," she complained. "There are an awful lot of legs and feet under those tables."

I was beginning to worry. Had Jackson's idea misfired? "Didn't anyone see any-thing?" I asked.

Lily and Olivia looked at each other, and Olivia nodded. "You tell," she said.

"There's a nasty little boy," Lily began, but Jackson interrupted her.

"Is he on the table near the door? Sitting next to a little girl in a pink velvet dress?"

Lily looked surprised. "Did you notice him too?"

"Yes. And Mel and I saw them in the shopping mall this afternoon," Jackson told her. "They're called Pipsy and Baby."

"Eugh! We don't want to help them," I said. "They were disgusting. There must be someone else."

I could tell Olivia didn't agree with me, even before she said, "I thought the little girl was very unhappy."

"Olivia's right. She IS unhappy." Sophie sounded very determined. "Her mum doesn't take any notice of her, except when she's telling her to look after Baby."

"I saw her little brother pinch her," Lily said. "He did it twice. He thought nobody was looking, but we were."

"She probably deserved it." I thought

of the way Pipsy had hung on to her mother's sleeve. "She whinges, and then she gets exactly what she wants. Honestly! It's true!" And I thought of something else. "You should see all the stuff their mum had bought them... Isn't that right, Jackson?"

Jackson didn't answer, and when I looked round she wasn't there.

"Where's she gone?" I asked, and I tried not to sound cross, even though I was – just a bit. We were supposed to be working together, but she'd slipped away without saying where she was going.

"She muttered something about presents," Sophie said, "and then she absolutely zoomed away."

Emma was frowning. "So what are we going to do?"

"Why don't we—" There was suddenly

such a loud noise from the dining room that
Madison never got to finish her sentence. We
ran to the door, and the children were jumping up and down, waving their arms in the air.

"We want Father Christmas!" they were
shouting. "Father Christmas! We want Father
Christmas!"

Baby was louder than any of them. "Want
Santa Claus! Want Santa Claus NOW!"

The adults were clearing away the chairs from one side of the hall, and it was obvious that something special was going to happen.

Lily was almost as wide-eyed as the waiting children. "What's going on?" she asked.

"Father Christmas is about to arrive," Madison told her. "I heard the grown-ups talking about it. Everyone's brought

presents for their children, they're going to be put in a big sack – and Father Christmas will give them out."

Lily sighed. "That's so brilliant."

"Hang on a minute." Ava was squinting into the distance. "Something's happening… Oh! It's Joe and Jenny's mum!"

"Children! CHILDREN!" Mrs Gibbs was clapping her hands for silence. "Father Christmas hasn't quite got here yet. He's looking for somewhere to park his reindeer, but he won't be long. Just give him another five minutes. Why don't you have some ice cream or an ice lolly while you're waiting?"

As a line of helpers carrying ice cream came out of the kitchen, the chidren settled down again. Only Baby stayed standing, but Pipsy whispered something in his ear, and

he sat back down in his chair with a flump. A moment later, Pipsy was given an ice lolly. She handed it to Baby, even though he was already holding a huge strawberry ice cream, and it was obvious that she'd bribed him to behave.

I was so surprised. She really did seem to be trying to look after him … so had I got it wrong? Again? I began to feel a little bit sick.

"We HAVE to do something about that kid," Sophie muttered.

"Hey! Guess what!" It was Jackson, and she was panting as if she'd been running. "Sophie said something that made me think, and I went to look in Baby's mum's shopping bags – and she was right! Every single toy was for Baby! All there was for Pipsy was a pink woolly hat and a couple of winter vests."

"Poor little girl!" Ava made a face. "That's so mean."

"But how can we help her?" Emma asked. "We can't exactly tell her mother off, can we?"

Jackson folded her arms. "WE can't. But the other mums and dads can!"

"But why would they?" Lily stared at her.

"That's what we're going to work out," Jackson said. "All of us together! Come on. What ideas do you have?"

Chapter Thirteen

I'd never seen so many blank faces all at once. Even Melody was looking at me as if I was mad, but to me it was obvious. If we could only get the other grown-ups to see the way Pipsy was treated, then surely they'd say something, and her mum would realise what she was doing.

The silence went on … and on … and on.

I was beginning to think it was a really stupid idea, but finally Olivia spoke. "Do you think Pipsy has a parcel in the sack?"

"She must have," Emma said. "Even her mother wouldn't be as wicked as that. It'd show her up in front of all the others…" She stopped. "Olivia! Are you thinking what I'm thinking?"

Olivia nodded. "Suppose we hid Pipsy's parcel!"

"I don't see how that would help." Melody was frowning.

Emma gave a little bounce of excitement. "Her mum would be shown up! Father Christmas is SURE to ask if every little boy and girl has had a present – and when Pipsy says, 'Not me!' EVERYONE will stare at her mother!"

"It's a brilliant idea," Madison said.

"Totally brilliant," Lily agreed.

Ava nodded. "What do you think, Jackson?"

I'd been secretly wishing I'd thought of the idea, but I gave myself a shake. We were all working together, weren't we? "Actually," I said, "I think it's really clever."

Sophie gave Olivia a hug. "Clever you."

"I'll go and find Pipsy's present," Melody said.

"Be careful," Madison warned her. "It's a real scrum all the way. You'll have to creep under the tables, and those kids have dropped food all over the floor." She held out her hands. "I'm horribly sticky!"

"I'll be fine," Melody told her, and she tapped her pendant and slid away.

"Fingers crossed," Ava said cheerfully, but at that moment the children's chatter faded into awed silence. The lights had dimmed, there was the sound of sleigh bells

... and into the room strode a tall Father Christmas, carrying an enormous sack.

"HO HO HO!" he bellowed. "Happy Christmas, everyone!"

"Oh NO!" Olivia clasped her hands in horror. "He's here already! How's Melody going to get the present?"

I didn't answer. I was watching to see what was going to happen next. The children were very quiet as Father Christmas dropped his sack on the floor and opened his arms wide.

"I said, HAPPY CHRISTMAS!" he shouted.

This time, the children knew what to do. "HAPPY CHRISTMAS!" they roared back.

"Who wants a present?"

"We do!"

Father Christmas nodded. "HO HO HO!"

"HO HO HO!" The children were so loud that I was amazed Father Christmas didn't go completely deaf. He actually seemed to like the noise; he beamed at everyone, pulled a chair towards him, and sat down, the bulging sack at his feet. "Let's see what we've got here, shall we?"

At once, Baby scrambled down from the table where he was sitting and began to push his way between the other children, elbowing them out of the way.

"Present for Baby!" he yelled. "Present for—" He stopped, and froze. His eyes bulged, and he

142

didn't say another word. He was right beside Jenny and Joe, and I could see them staring at him in astonishment.

"Well done, Sophie." Madison was chuckling loudly. "I'd love to know what she's saying to him!"

"SOPHIE?" I hadn't noticed that she'd slipped away. I squinted my eyes, and Madison was right. I could just make out a shadowy Sophie behind Baby, and she was whispering in his ear.

Baby opened his mouth as if he was going to scream – but he didn't. Instead he meekly turned around, and made his way back to his seat. Every so often he looked nervously over his shoulder. I could understand why.

At the side of the room Father Christmas had opened up the sack, and was pulling out a handful of parcels. I held my breath, but it was OK. The presents were for other children; there was nothing for Pipsy yet. I couldn't see Melody, but as the children came hurrying up to collect their gifts I saw the sack twitch as if someone was rooting about in it.

She needs help, I thought, and at the same

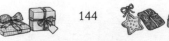

moment Lily whispered in my ear, "Watch this! We're going to give Melody a bit more time!" And then she tapped her pendant and was gone, and so was Olivia … and a moment later the net of balloons that had been hidden on the balcony burst open. Dozens of brightly coloured balloons drifted down, and the children shouted with laughter and jumped on their chairs to try and catch them.

Several balloons had a life of their own and floated right across the room ... and I was almost sure Madison, Ava and Emma had something to do with that.

Father Christmas smiled, shrugged, and sat down to wait while Mrs Gibbs and the other helpers tried to sort out the chaos. Nobody would have heard him even if he had tried to keep going; the noise was indescribable ... and I'm certain as certain can be that neither he nor any of the grown-ups noticed as I skidded to a halt beside the sack, and tipped the presents on the floor in a heap.

"What are you DOING?" Melody hissed.

"It's OK," I whispered. "Nobody's looking! Quick! Where's Pipsy's present?"

Chapter Fourteen

I thought Jackson was mad when she emptied out the sack, but she was right. It took us only a second to find the present. We grabbed it, shoved the other presents back, and ran.

"That was COOL!" Ava said as we arrived back in the doorway, panting. "What's Pipsy got?"

"I don't know," Jackson said, "but there's no way it's a fluffy purple dog."

We looked at the sad little parcel. It was small, and very flat ... as if it was a hankie, or a scarf.

"Oh dear," I said. "Poor Pipsy."

Olivia and Lily had made their way back from the balcony, and I could feel Olivia looking at me in surprise.

I swallowed hard. "You were right, and I was wrong about her. You don't need to say anything."

"I wasn't going to," she said, and she smiled at me. "Look! Father Christmas is standing up again!"

"HO HO HO!" said Father Christmas. "Sorry about that little interruption, kiddies! Now, let's see who's next?"

It was really hard waiting until all the presents were given out. Baby had the biggest parcel of all, but after he'd ripped off the paper and had a quick glance at the very expensive aeroplane inside, he dropped it on the floor. He turned to Pipsy, and I'm

148

sure he pinched her because she gave a little squeal and her eyes filled with tears.

Sophie was beside me, and I heard her sigh. "He's SO horrible."

"What did you say to him?" Madison wanted to know.

"I told him I was a Christmas fairy, and if he didn't sit down and be quiet he wouldn't

get any presents at all," Sophie said with grim satisfaction.

When the final child had trailed back to his seat, Father Christmas turned the sack inside out, and looked around. "There we go, kiddlywinks! I haven't left anyone out, have I? Everyone's got something lovely?"

"Come on, Pipsy!" Madison whispered, and we waited, holding our breath … but Pipsy said nothing.

Nothing at all.

Father Christmas began folding up the sack. "Then that's all right, my dears—"

"NO!"

It was Baby, and he was even redder in the face than usual. "PRESENT! Where's Pipsy's present? Pipsy hasn't got a present!"

I nearly collapsed. Whatever was going on? Our plan – it was SO not working!

 150

There was a murmur from the grown–
ups, and I saw Baby's mother stand up.

"That's my DARLING boy!" she called
out. "SUCH a loving brother! And he's quite
right. My little girl hasn't had anything yet!"

The woman sitting next to her said
loudly, "And you didn't notice? REALLY!
It's a good thing your little boy did!"

"He's the sweetest thing," his mother said
proudly, but at that moment the sweetest
thing climbed down from the table and
began to push his way through the children. His lower lip stuck out, and he was
scowling terribly. He stomped in between
the tables, and plonked himself in front of
Father Christmas.

"Want Pipsy's present!" he said. "Want it
NOW!"

"HO HO HO, young man." Father

Christmas sat down. "Why don't you go and fetch your sister? I'm sure her present's somewhere here." He looked hopefully at the rows of grown-ups. "Has anyone seen it?"

Baby was gradually turning puce. "Don't WANT to fetch Pipsy! Want Pipsy's PRESENT! Pipsy promised!"

Father Christmas stroked his beard. He was obviously puzzled. "But—"

"STUPID Santa!" Baby stamped his foot. "Pipsy promised! Pipsy said I could have her fluffy wuffy dog! She PROMISED!"

The grown-ups were now muttering quite loudly. The bossy woman next to Pipsy's mother asked, very clearly, "DID you bring a present for your little girl?"

"Of course I did!" Pipsy's mum sounded defensive.

Baby heard her, and glared. "Where fluffy

wuffy dog, Mumsy wumsy? Where Pipsy's fluffy wuffy dog that does singing?"

"Father Christmas isn't giving Pipsy a fluffy dog, Baby darling. He's going to give her a sweet little hankie—"

Baby's scream made Father Christmas jump.

And then Pipsy was screaming too. Every single child and adult in the room stared and stared as she screamed at the top of her voice, "But you PROMISED, Mumsy! You PROMISED you'd buy me the purple fluffy dog and I said Baby could have it because he keeps on and on and on pinching me and he said he'd never ever EVER pinch me again if I gave it to him – even though it's my very best present!"

"REALLY!" The bossy woman was totally horrified.

154

But Pipsy's mum banged her fist on the table. "I didn't promise! I never said I'd buy a purple—"

And then Jackson's voice rang out, loud and clear. "Yes, you did."

Chapter Fifteen

I'd had enough. Someone had to stand up for Pipsy.

I shut my eyes, and I muttered the words of the Growing Spell.

> "I wish to grow,
> To make things right.
> I wish to be
> My normal height!"

I waited for the weird whooshing feeling but nothing happened. I grabbed Melody. "QUICK! We've got to tell everyone that we heard her! We heard her promise!"

Melody screwed up her eyes and began to mutter the spell, but yet again nothing happened.

"Oh NO!" I wailed.

And then Olivia – Olivia! – gave me a massive push. "Go ON!" she hissed. "WE'LL say the spell! Go ON!"

So I did. I tapped my pendant, and walked back into the room … and Melody came with me … and suddenly the air was filled with tiny twinkly stars. None of the adults seemed to notice; only Baby's eyes grew wide as they clung to our hair, our clothes, our faces and our arms … and then they were gone, and we were standing in front of Pipsy's mum looking totally normal.

"We were in the shopping mall," I said, "and we heard you! Me and my friend – we both did. You promised you'd buy Pipsy a purple fluffy dog that sings and goes round in circles—"

"You DID, Mumsy!" Pipsy was crying now. "You DID!"

"YES! MY fluffy dog!" Baby was not only stamping his feet, he was actually trying to punch Father Christmas. "Want it NOW!"

Pipsy and Baby's mum stood up, then sank back in her chair, her head in her hands.

"I hope you're ashamed of yourself." The bossy woman was glaring at her. "Just look what you've done!"

"FLUFFY DOG!" Baby was rolling on the floor. The children were open-mouthed, and the grown-ups were staring…

"Stop it, Georgie." The voice came from the other side of the room, and every head turned to see who had spoken. A tall man was standing by the door, wearing a coat and scarf, and carrying a suitcase.

Baby was suddenly very still, but Pipsy

wriggled down from the table and rushed towards him. "DADDY!" She flung herself at him, and he lifted her up and hugged her.

"What's going on?" he asked.

"Nothing, Daddy." Pipsy buried her head in his coat.

Her father looked at Baby, and raised his eyebrows. "Georgie?"

Baby opened his mouth, shut it again, and looked wildly round at me and Melody. "Go away, Christmas Fairies! Go AWAY!"

"What?" His father frowned. "Georgie, have you been pinching Pipsy?"

Georgie drooped. "Yes, Daddy."

His father strode across the room, and grabbed him. "We're going to go home right now this minute. Leila? Are you ready?"

Pipsy and Georgie's mum came hurrying towards him. "Baby's only little," she began.

160

But her husband held up his hand. "He's nearly four, Leila. He's not a baby any more." He set off for the door, then paused. "I'm so sorry," he told Father Christmas. "I apologise for my badly behaved son." He swung Pipsy onto his shoulders, and smiled up at her. "It's not long until Christmas Eve, sweetie. You'd

better start thinking of a name for the fluffy purple dog Father Christmas is going to bring you…"

And off they went.

"HO HO HO!" Father Christmas was beaming at us. "Well done, girls. Well done!" And he began to clap, and everyone else joined in, and then they began cheering. We didn't know where to look – the dining room was positively shaking – but then brightly coloured stars began drifting down from the ceiling, and there was a sudden hush.

"Jackson! Melody!"

I turned round and so did Melody – and we saw Fairy Mary, Miss Scritch and Fairy Fifibelle Lee outlined in the doorway. Fairy Fifibelle Lee was clapping, Miss Scritch was beckoning and Fairy Mary was pointing … pointing at my necklace.

I put my hand up to my neck.

 162

Melody saw what I was doing, and she gasped. "JACKSON!" she said. "You've got SIX STARS! Oh, have I? Have I got six stars too?"

I looked … and she had.

"WOWSERS!" we shouted, and to the complete and utter astonishment of every single person in The Nag's Head we danced up and

down and up and down and round and round
before running out of the room … and if it
wasn't cool, I don't care.

And neither did Melody.

Chapter Sixteen

So that's how Jackson and I finally got our six stars, and became – at long last – fully qualified Stargirls.

The other Stargirls were waiting for us. They'd grown back to their usual height, and I thought we were all totally visible, but when Mrs Gibbs hurried after us and looked down the corridor I heard her say, "How strange! There's nobody here! And I wanted to say how brave they were to stand up for that little girl!"

I looked at Fairy Mary, and she winked at me. "How does it feel to be a Stargirl, Melody?" she said.

"WONDERFUL!" I said, and then I added, "But it would never EVER have happened without the others."

"Especially Olivia," Jackson said, and she actually gave Olivia a hug. "Thanks."

"It was nothing," Olivia told her, but it was easy to see that she was really pleased.

Jackson gave Fairy Mary a cheeky grin. "So, are we the best at making mistakes, Fairy Mary? The very best?"

Fairy Mary didn't answer, but she put her arms around our shoulders as we made our way out of the garden door, and over to the Travelling Tower.

We all piled in, and we were back at the Academy in no time at all.

Miss Scritch led us into the sitting room. "Please sit down," she said.

So we did.

166

And I suddenly remembered sitting in that very same room when we very first came to the Fairy Mary McBee Academy for Stargirls. Jackson and I hadn't even been sure if we'd wanted to be there ... but we'd stayed.

And now ... now we were actual Stargirls!

As Fairy Mary McBee solemnly handed me my certificate, and I heard the sound of music starting up next door, I thought how lucky I was. I was a Stargirl, I had six other friends as well as Jackson, there was an amazing party just about to start – and it was nearly Christmas.

YEAH!!!!!!

Jackson Williams

Loves:
Learning new spells

Hates:
Gushy pet names

Good at:
Magic

Favourite colour:
Purple

Starsign:
Capricorn

Melody Weston

Starsign:
Scorpio

Loves:
Sausage
rolls

Hates:
Not being
in charge

**Favourite
colour:**
Red

**Most
proud of:**
Getting her
6th star!

Melody and Jackson's Christmas Scrambler

Can you unscramble the words below and then find them in the wordsearch?

WLOKESAFN......................................

ESTAF......................................

INEICPSME ....

TROGTO ....

DERNEIRE......................................

RIWTNATS ....

ASMWNON ....

ETSNSRPE ....

HTRIGLSAT......................................

```
N O O F Z R E P I G N K X O A
A J T E Q E V V R T G A L B A
M D T A A M E E L W T F G O K
W V O S C B I S W H Z N T K O
O P R T Y N Z E G H S U W C A
N N G W D Z M I N C D T I V E
S I S E X B L P R K T K N E K
Z L E V H R P E Q S Z L S H A
H R E Q A W T C S C A L T P L
A A G T U D Z N G T K L A H F
C Q S H K M E I O S H U R Q W
D L V P T Z B M H U T L Z H O
C W C K T H I M S C M Y S J N
P Y S T N E S E R P F G R D S
M O D L U S M G A L Z N E M R
```

4

Stargirl Academy

Ava's
Sparkling Spell

VIVIAN FRENCH

FREE GIFT
Tokens inside

5

Stargirl Academy

Emma's
Glittering Spell

VIVIAN FRENCH

FREE GIFT
Tokens inside

6

Stargirl Academy

Olivia's
Twinkling Spell

VIVIAN FRENCH

FREE GIFT
Tokens inside

Collect them all!

Stargirl Academy

Where magic makes a difference!

Emma   Madison   Sophie   Ava   Lily   Olivia

Melody   Jackson

Visit

www.stargirlacademy.com

to get your free poster of Melody and Jackson!

IMAGE AND COGNITION

This book is gratefully dedicated to MYC